Finders Keepers

by

Ann Halam

Published in 2004 in Great Britain by
Barrington Stoke Ltd, Sandeman House, Trunk's Close,
55 High Street, Edinburgh EH1 1SR

ISBN 1-842992-03-1

Printed in Great Britain by Bell & Bain Ltd

A Note from the Author

My father never had a metal detector, but he used to spend a lot of time tinkering with our old car, when I was the age that Val is in the story, and I liked to watch. I didn't help much, I just handed him a spanner now and then. There were no green fields where I lived in Manchester, but near our garage there was a strange patch of waste ground where some houses had been bombed in the Second World War. It was supposed to be dangerous. We children weren't supposed to dig for treasure there, but we did. Once we found some cow's teeth and once the shell of a tortoise. We didn't ever find anything as exciting as a statue of Cassandra, though.

Cassandra really was the name of a Trojan Princess who was taken from Troy after the Trojans were defeated in the Trojan War. She was cursed with the gift of prophecy, or so the story goes. She kept telling people that disaster would fall, and nobody believed her. Hector was the name of a Trojan hero, and Achilles (Akili in modern Greek) was the Greek champion who defeated him. Maybe things turn out differently, this time ...

Contents

Chapter 1
The Finders

Val's dad was a treasure hunter. He loved to go out with his metal detector and look for old metal in the woods and fields outside town.

Sometimes he found old coins or buttons and bits of old tools. But it was like fishing – he and his mates didn't seem to mind if they never found much. What they wanted to do was mess about outside for hours on end, and try out their metal-detecting gadgets.

Val thought it was a total joke. But if she didn't have anything to do on a Saturday afternoon, she would sometimes go out with Dad. It was nice to do something with him. It made her feel nice and calm.

One cold spring day, Dad and one of his treasure-hunting mates were doing their detecting – looking for treasure, that is – in a big, empty field that had just been ploughed. Val was sitting on a gate, watching them. Dad called Val over.

Dad passed her his metal detector. "Hold the Garrett for me, love."

Val took it. Dad's metal detector looked like a pancake on a green metal pole. There were controls halfway up the pole and a screen at the top. While she held the Garrett, Dad and Charlie bent over the small screen of Charlie's gadget. It was a Sonic Soil Disturbance Locator and Charlie had just got it. It was his newest toy. Charlie was the

one who had all the expensive stuff.
He bought everything he saw in the *Metal
Detector News*.

"That's *got* to be a wall trace," said Dad.

"Got to be!" said fat Charlie, pulling up his
old torn trousers and tugging on the ear flaps
of his tatty old cap. Charlie spent money on
gadgets, but not on clothes. He was excited
now.

Val looked. All she could see was the grey
screen with dots all over it. Then she saw
something sticking out of the earth in front
of her.

She laid the Garrett metal detector
carefully on the ground, and got down for a
closer look. There was a *toe* sticking out of
the pale brown earth. It was black, and very
small, but it looked so real that it gave her a
creepy feeling.

When she touched it, she was glad it felt like stone, not flesh.

Dad and Charlie had started a mobile phone chat with their mates about what it was they could see on that screen.

Val brushed away the loose soil until she could see properly what she had found. It was about 20cm high – a statue of a woman in a long dress, sitting on a chair. Most of the chair was hidden by her dress. She was holding something like a big plate, upright in her lap.

Val was impressed. She didn't think Dad or any of them had ever found a statue. But she still had a creepy feeling. She rubbed the soil from the black stone face, and jumped when she found two red eyes staring back at her.

"Hey!" she shouted. "Dad! I've found something!"

Dad and Charlie were excited, and very jealous. Dad called his mates at once on his mobile.

"We've got a strike in the Blue Room, you guys!"

The gang always gave marks from one to ten for the things they found. A strike meant ten marks. It was the best you could get. The "Blue Room" was the code name for this field, on a farm called Seven Hills.

When they talked on their mobile phones they used code. Charlie said if they didn't use code, other treasure hunters might listen in and spy on them.

Charlie and Dad used Charlie's electronic ruler to measure every bit of the statue.

They checked the place where it had been lying with the Garrett and the Sonic Soil Disturbance Locator.

"Looks as if it was buried in a wooden box," said Dad. "The box has rotted away, but I'm getting strong traces of iron. There might have been an iron lock, or perhaps the box had metal bands round it."

"What do you mean, 'might'?" Val wanted to know. "Aren't you going to dig?"

"Not right now," said Dad. "It's time we got back to the clubhouse."

"We've got to get this baby out of sight," said Charlie, looking around with a scowl. "You can't be too careful, Val. There are other metal-detectorists about. And they aren't as honest as we are. If they know we've found a rich site, they'll be right in here!"

Charlie and Dad wrapped the statue up. They kept on looking round all the time, as if they thought that those other wicked treasure hunters were going to jump out of the hedge.

They put the statue in Charlie's backpack, and set off for the clubhouse, which was an old hut on the edge of a golf course. The hut didn't belong to the treasure hunters but nobody used it any more. One of the gang was a member of the golf club so the club let them have it for free.

It was raining by the time they got there. Big Sal, the biker, and her little thin friend Kerry were waiting outside, like soldiers on watch.

"Come on," said Big Sal, "indoors, quick."

"No trouble?" asked Dad, with a wink.

"No hostiles sighted. No-one around," said Kerry. "Not as yet."

They're like kids, thought Val. *Who do they think they are? Commandos?*

The inside of the little hut was already full of treasure hunters. They sat on old garden chairs and empty boxes. Mrs Pritty, the member of the golf club, was very prim and proper. She was boiling a kettle on a camping stove. Young Dave and Old Scottish Dave had the teapot and the mugs set out.

On the wall there was a map of the local area. The places where they had already looked for treasure were marked in different colours. Under the map was a huge stack of metal detector catalogues and hobby magazines.

Big Sal, Kerry, Charlie, Dad and Val squeezed in to join the party. Charlie Woo took out the statue. Everyone stared at it in amazement, and Val couldn't help feeling proud.

"It might be modern," said Young Dave at last. "How can you tell?"

"It's *not* modern," said Charlie. "It's lasted well, that's all. Bet you any money it's real you-know-what. Bet you 50p."

"Now, lads, no gambling! I won't have it!" said Mrs Pritty. "Let's not fall into Satan's wicked ways. Young Dave, you can pour the tea."

"If it *is* real, then this is proof!" said Young Dave.

"Proof of what?" asked Val.

Dad gave a warning cough, looked at Young Dave and shook his head. He rubbed his hands together. "Well, well, a cup of tea. That would be nice."

"Let's have a sandwich swap," said Charlie, with a wink at Dad and Young Dave. "Come on, everybody. Onto the important stuff. Let's see what sandwiches you've all got. Mine's a tuna and red pepper."

The treasure hunters were an odd bunch.

Big Sal was covered in tattoos, wore old motorbike leathers and often looked as if she'd been in a fight.

Her sharp-faced little friend Kerry kept a knife in her boot, which she liked to show to people.

Mrs Pritty had other strong ideas as well as thinking gambling was the Devil's work. She kept photos of her 15 parrots in her bag, instead of photos of her grandchildren. She said the parrots were more interesting.

Then there was Charlie, who spent his money on gadgets, and dressed like a tramp.

Young Dave was clever – he was in a band and he was writing a book about Jamaica. But he couldn't hold down a job.

Old Scottish Dave kept the map up-to-date with new marks and colourings and he wrote down whatever they found in his big black notebook. But he lived in a hostel and had a problem with drink.

The only thing they all had in common, besides their dreams, was that each of them had plenty of spare time.

Val's dad did, too. He had been a roofer, until he fell off the fire station and hurt his back. Now he only worked part-time for the council. It didn't matter. Val's mum made lots of money from her mail-order company. Val sometimes tried to get her mum to make Dad give up treasure hunting. Val thought if Dad had a different hobby he might have smart friends, instead of these nice-but-nutty losers.

But it was no use. "Your dad's happy," said Mum. "That's all I care about."

Young Dave poured the tea, while everyone put their sandwiches in a pile on Mrs Pritty's paper plates. Big Sal and Kerry had huge cheese and pickle sandwiches the size of doorsteps. Everyone fancied those. Mrs Pritty's sandwiches were smoked salmon with cream cheese. They all praised those, too. Old Scottish Dave would not put his sausage and ketchup baps into the swap and there was a bit of a row. The tuna and red pepper were the stars of the show.

They seemed to have lost all interest in the statue. Val knew it was because there was something going on – something that they didn't want to talk about. Not while Val was listening. Something to do with that field they called the "Blue Room". *They're kids in grown-up bodies*, she thought. *As if I care about their secrets.*

She sipped her tea, ate a sandwich, and thought about her cat, Nippy, who was going to have kittens very soon. If there was a ginger one, Val was going to try and get Mum and Dad to let her keep it. The statue stood beside her, staring at her with those red eyes. It was getting on her nerves. In the end she had to pick it up. She found a rag, and started cleaning away the rest of the soil.

The woman had curly hair, tied on top of her head. The plate she was holding in her lap had a pattern around the edge, and a hole like an open mouth in the middle ... but the woman's own mouth was covered. There was a bandage tied around it like a gag, carved into the black stone.

"That's *weird*," muttered Val.

The statue was beautiful. It was carved so carefully that you could see every detail, and it was perfect. There were no chips, no broken parts, no cracks. But it was still giving Val the creeps.

There was a name on the base in capital letters: CASSANDRA. *That must be her name*, thought Val. There was soil packed inside the mouth-hole on the big plate.

Val picked at it with her fingernail, and a voice spoke in her head.

First will be snow white, that will not live a day,

Then the black female, screeching like the owl,

Black with white will follow,

Then the golden fawn comes, on rosy feet.

She must have yelped in surprise. The treasure hunters all stared at her.

"What's up, Val?" said her dad. "Did your dark lady bite you?"

"N-no ...! Look, she has a bandage round her mouth, isn't that weird?"

"Have you been cleaning it, Val?" said Scottish Dave. "You shouldn't do that. Not until we know what it's made of. It might need some special cleaning stuff."

Dad laughed. "It looks tough enough to me. Never tell a teenager off for doing a spot

14

of cleaning, Dave. But, come to think of it, I'll put her in my kitbag." He looked around. "Oh, better get it on record. Do we agree that this fine strike belongs to the collection of Tony and Val Hector? And Val can take her home?"

Tony was Val's dad's name, and their surname was Hector.

"The club says *aye*," said Mrs Pritty. The rest of them nodded. "Aye," they said in chorus. Scottish Dave got out the notebook, and wrote down the details. In code, of course.

"Don't spread the news, Tony," he warned. "Keep your mouths shut, all right?"

Exactly like kids, thought Val. But as she handed her find over to Dad, she couldn't resist poking her finger into the mouth-hole again. At once, the voice in her mind came back.

First will be snow white, that will not live a day …

"What on earth's going on?" she whispered to herself.

Whatever it was, it didn't feel good.

Chapter 2
The Kittens

Val and her dad got a lift with Mrs Pritty, who dropped them at the corner of their street. Mum had bought Dad a new Porsche, which he loved. But driving hurt his back, so mostly it stayed parked in the street.

The moment they walked in the door, Val's Mum rushed out of the living room, big smiles all over her face.

"What's up, Jackie?" said Dad. "Have you made another million-pound deal?"

"No! She's had them! Mother and babies are doing well!"

"Oh, great!" cried Val, wishing she'd stayed at home. "How many are there? How long did it take? Is there a ginger one?"

Nippy was lying in a cardboard box on a piece of old blanket and layers of newspaper, next to a radiator. Her slim black body was curled tenderly around four blobs of fur.

They hardly looked like kittens – they looked more like big mice. One of them, a little black one, was wriggling and squeaking, kicking at the big ginger one. The other two were quiet. The black and white one was sucking away. Nippy licked at the white one, which was lying between her front paws.

It seemed to be asleep.

Val bent over the box, forgetting everything but these little miracles. She'd never seen newborn kittens before. It put the statue right out of her head.

"Don't touch them, love," warned her mum. "A mother cat doesn't like you to touch her kittens."

Dad got down, too, and stroked Nippy's head. "You're a fine mum, aren't you, Nips?" The cat looked up at him, and gave a proud mew.

"The white one was born first," said Mum. "But I'm worried about it – it doesn't seem as healthy as the others."

"It'll be OK, I'm sure," said Dad. "The mother cat will know best."

Val phoned her friend, Nessa, and she came round after dinner. Val had promised Nessa one of Nippy's kittens.

The two girls knelt and peered into the box.

"You get first choice," said Val.

"Are you sure? Then I want the black one. Is it a girl? I hope it's a girl."

"I don't know," said Val, with a sigh of relief. It would have been hard to give up the ginger one. "We can find out in a few days, but we can't touch them yet."

Nessa's tiny black one was fighting with the big ginger kitten again. They were blind and helpless, but strong and fit.

"I'm going to call her Owl. Listen to the way she screeches."

Something clicked in Val's mind, something she should remember but she didn't know why. "You can't call her Owl. That's not a girl's name."

"So?" said Nessa. "Get a grip. That's a cat, not a girl, Val. Oh, look at the ginger one, look at his rosy-pink little *feet*. I can see his claws! Like tiny fish hooks!"

20

"Cats have paws, not feet," said Val. "I'm going to call the ginger one Fawn. It seems like his name. That's if my mum and dad let me keep him—"

Something clicked in her mind again. Then the words came back –

First will be snow white, that will not live a day,

Then the black female, screeching like the owl,

Black with white will follow,

Then the golden fawn comes, on rosy feet.

Nessa laughed. "A fawn is a baby *deer*, you dork. You can't call a cat that."

Val wasn't listening. She turned her head. Across the room was the display case that held Dad's best finds. There were Victorian glass medicine bottles, blue and green and clear. There were old lumps of machinery fused with rust. His Roman coins lay in a velvet tray with his 800-year-old penny.

The new statue stood alone, gleaming like ebony. Mum had washed it and polished it before dinner.

The grim red eyes were staring straight at Val.

Cold chills went down her spine.

Snow white will not live a day, said the voice in her head.

Black with white will live one year,

Then the roaring wheels will slay.

Black Owl will have a longer span, but die in pain, when …

"NO!" yelled Val, slamming her hands over her ears, and shutting her eyes tight. "*Stop it*! I don't want to know!"

"Val?" cried Nessa. "What's up with you?"

Val opened her eyes and dropped her hands. The voice had stopped.

"I don't know," she said. "Someone walked over my grave." She gave a shrug. "Forget it ... I think we should leave the kittens with their mum now. D'you want to come up to my room?"

"No," said Nessa. "I've got to get ready. I'm seeing Tez tonight."

Oh dear, thought Val.

Nessa's boyfriend didn't know it yet, but he was in trouble ... Tez, whose real name was Terry, was Young Dave the treasure hunter's brother. Young Dave had told Val's dad that Tez was seeing someone else. Val's dad had told Nessa.

Dad didn't mean any harm – he just didn't want Nessa to get hurt. But it would have been better if he'd kept quiet. Nessa had a

23

fierce temper, and now it was all going to come out.

When Nessa had gone, Val went to the display case.

She opened the glass doors. She couldn't seem to help herself.

Her fingertip touched the mouth-hole in that big plate.

The voice spoke in Val's head.

There will be blows and broken jewels,

Blood will flow in the tracks. The music will be silenced.

Love ends in tears and shame.

"Oh my God," whispered Val.

She backed away from the statue and wiped her finger on her jeans.

She'd only touched clean, cold stone, but her whole hand felt dirty.

"I don't want this. What's happening to me?"

The gift is given by fate not choice,

Doom falls. Doom. Doom. Dreadful doom upon this house.

"SHUT UP!" hissed Val, gritting her teeth.

"Shut up with your stupid doom. You're only a statue. Leave me alone. You don't know anything."

It is on its way. Doom. Destruction. Terrible things.

"Shut up! I'm not listening to you!"

Val went back to the kittens with her hands over her ears.

Nippy sniffed at the weak white one, and mewed.

It was lying apart from the others. It was getting chilled.

Chapter 3
The Museum

Mum and Dad and Val stayed up half the night with the white kitten.

They took it out of the box and tried to keep it warm on a hot water bottle wrapped in a scarf. Mum fed it warm milk from a dropper. But the poor thing died at about 2 a.m.

Val went into school the next day feeling upset.

The first person she saw was Tez, lurking by the hall. His left eye was half shut, with a big puffy bruise round it.

When he saw Val he walked away fast, without even saying hi.

Ooh, this looks bad, she thought.

Nessa came in late, and sat down by Val.

"How'd it go last night?" said Val. As if she needed to ask.

"*Awful*," said Nessa. "We went out, to the Torch ..."

The Torch was a club. Val had never been there, and she didn't really want to go. Tez and Nessa both looked a lot older than 15, so they could get past the door.

"That girl was there. The one your dad told me about. So we ... we left. We went to my house, and we had a *terrible* fight." Nessa had begun to cry now. "I pulled my spiky earrings out, the ones Tez gave me for Christmas, so hard I tore my earlobe." Nessa pushed back her long blonde hair so Val could see one ear, taped up with a plaster.

"I threw them at him, and then I … I hit him really hard. I was so *mad*. Tez got mad, too, and started smashing m … my CDs. He cut his hand, and got blood all over the place, an' then my mum came in and yelled at us. She said she had a good mind to call the police and get us both a night in the cells. It was horrible. I didn't know I could be like that. I'm *so* ashamed."

Nessa tugged a CD without a case out of her bag. It was covered in scratches and ugly patches of dried blood.

"This is what all my CDs are like. Ruined. Like my life."

There will be blows and broken jewels. Blood on the tracks …

29

Val felt so scared, she began to feel tears in her own eyes.

First the white kitten, and now this!

Nessa gave her a hug. "Don't *you* cry, Val. It's not your fault."

Then Mr Webber, the form tutor, came in and they had to sit quiet. But Val felt so weird, she kept away from Nessa for the rest of the day.

That statue has to go, she thought. *This is driving me nuts.*

The next Saturday there was a "Finder's Day" at the museum in town. People could bring their treasures and someone from the museum would tell them if they were valuable, or just junk.

Dad took the black statue along, and Val went with him. She didn't want to explain why she hated that thing.

There was a long queue at the front desk. They had to fill in a form and wait to be called. At last it was their turn.

Dad went boldly up to the desk, took his parcel out of his kit bag, and unwrapped it. He stood the statue on the desk.

The curator from the museum looked it over. "This is very interesting!" he said.

"That writing, on the base. Is it her name?" asked Val. "Who's Cassandra?"

"Hmm. Cassandra was a princess from the city of Troy. The Greeks carried her off to Greece. She had the gift of seeing into the future, but she was cursed by the gods. She could foretell the future, but nobody would believe her."

"Did she only tell bad things?" Val wanted to know.

"She foretold disasters, yes." The curator was a thin man with sandy hair. He took out a magnifying glass, and looked at the statue closely. "Did you notice that there's more writing, around the rim of the shield she's holding? *Rei Obscurii Dico*. The language is Latin, of course. It means *I speak of hidden things*."

"That's funny," said Dad. "She can't speak. Her mouth's all wrapped up."

"I thought what she was holding was a mask," said Val, "or a big plate."

"No, this is a warrior's shield," said the curator. Val liked him. He wasn't stuck-up or snooty. He was just doing his job. His grey eye looked very big through the magnifying glass. He put it down.

"This is a very fine, interesting little figure. May I ask how you came by it?"

"I could have bought it from a junk shop," said Val's dad.

"I see. How much did you pay for her, if you don't mind my asking?"

"Might have been fifty quid. I liked the look of her."

"Well, you've done very well, Mr Hector." The curator tapped the stone lady on the head with his finger. "I think this is a late Roman work, which could fetch five hundred or a thousand pounds at auction. If you can leave it with me, I'll get an expert on Roman statues to look at it."

Val wondered what would happen if, by mistake, the curator put his finger into the hole in the mask ... or shield. Would he hear Cassandra's voice? What would he find out? Something he didn't want to know, that was for sure.

"Roman," said Dad. "That's what I thought. Thanks very much." He took the statue out of the man's hands and quickly wrapped it up again. "Don't worry about showing her to anyone else. We don't want to sell her, do we, Val?"

Dad rushed Val out of the museum. "Dad!" she yelled, as soon as they were outside on the pavement. "Why did you tell those lies?"

Dad grinned. "I wasn't lying, love. Just being careful."

"I bet I know what this is about. I *thought* you were all being strange about the statue the other day. You didn't ask the farmer if you could search that field!"

You were always meant to ask the owner before you went metal detecting on private land. Then you had to report any finds of value.

"You don't want anyone to know you found something valuable!"

Dad winked at her, and started walking. "You've got it, sweetheart."

"*Dad!* You can't do this. We can't keep the statue. It's stealing!"

Dad stopped. He didn't look guilty at all. "Listen, love. If you must know, we think there's a whole Roman ruin under there. We'll do the right thing. We'll tell the farmer, and pay him his share. But we don't want the news getting about until we've had a proper look for ourselves. Treasure hunting is cut-throat work."

"The curator said it was worth a thousand pounds. We should sell it!"

"He said five hundred," said Dad. "Always believe the lower sum, love. Then you won't get let down," he laughed. "We can't sell her. Like you said – that would be stealing. This way, we're just *keeping* her for a while. Come on, Val. How can you want to sell such a great find? What's got into you? We don't need the money!"

Dad marched off, humming a tune. Val gave a big sigh. Dad could be stubborn, and he wasn't going to change his mind. She trailed after him, too upset to talk.

Chapter 4
The Terrible Shock

Mum had started working for a mail-order company when Dad broke his back and was so ill. At first she'd been in telesales, making phone calls. It was easy because she could make the phone calls from home. She had become a manager, and then a local area director of the firm. She had done very well. The Hectors still lived in the same little house, but everything was perfect. The garden was a showcase. Dad and Mum both had beautiful new cars. They had all the new

clothes and treats they wanted, and they
went for fabulous holidays.

Val never thought about where the money
came from. All she knew was that Mum
worked for a company called *Floral Magic*.
The spare bedroom was always full of boxes
of samples, and the whiff of apple blossom or
roses sometimes filled the house. She didn't
really know what her mum did.

Maybe Dad didn't know much about it
either.

Val had noticed that Mum was getting
visits from someone called Mr Marcos.
He was a businessman with a big dark car and
an expensive coat and gold rings on his
fingers. Val had wondered what went on in
these "business meetings". Mum was always
in a strange mood after them. Could Mum
and Mr Marcos be having an affair? But Mr
Marcos was a fat, middle-aged man with piggy

little eyes. Anyway, Val didn't believe her mum would ever cheat on Dad.

She didn't suspect the truth, and nor did Dad, until the terrible shock came.

It happened on a Monday. Val came home thinking this was the day she'd get Mum and Dad to say she could keep Fawn. *I'll get him to do something really cute*, she thought, *and make sure they're watching*. She was sure they'd say yes. They were as soft in the head about the kittens as Val was. She dumped her school bag and her jacket, and walked happily into the dining room, which was the room where Mum did her office stuff.

"Hi, I'm home ..."

There was a pile of papers and open files spread over the polished oak table. Mum loved that table. It was her pride and joy. Mum and Dad were sitting there. Val's heart started to thump. Mum was still in her dressing gown, and her face was like something in a horror movie. Her eyes were wild, tears streamed down her cheeks.

"*Mum! Dad!* What's wrong? Oh God, what's happened—?"

"There's nothing w-wrong," said Mum. "Just leave us for a bit, love."

Val sat down, because her knees were giving way. "What is it?" she gasped. "*Please*, you've got to tell me! Is someone dead? Is it Grandma Melrose?"

Her mum's mum had been ill, but it was only 'flu.

In her mind she heard the awful voice of the statue, promising horrors –

Doom. Terrible things.

"Your gran's OK," said Mum. "It's nothing like that, Val. Please, could you just leave us alone for a bit?"

"She's got to know some time," said Dad. "Will you tell her, love, or will I?"

Mum took a deep breath. "I'll tell her. You're right, Tony. I should tell her."

It took Mum a while to get the story out.

She had done very well with *Floral Magic*, for a few years. That much was true. When she'd stopped making such good money, she hadn't had the heart to tell Val and Dad. She'd started running up debts, getting credit cards that Dad knew nothing about, and making sure he never saw the statements. She'd been able to carry on as if there was still plenty of money. In the end, there had been Mr Marcos.

Mr Marcos worked for a finance company that had taken on Mum's credit card debts. Mum thought it was a magic way out. Instead of paying out lots of different sums of money to all the credit card accounts, Mum only had to make one payment, to Mr Marcos, once a month. His company paid Mum's credit cards for her. If Mum couldn't find the whole amount, she simply owed Mr Marcos more money next time.

Then disaster had struck. *Floral Magic* had gone bust, and Mum had been left with almost nothing. For the last two months she hadn't been able to pay Mr Marcos. He'd said he'd wait for her to find some more work. But then today he'd come to tell her things had changed. She had to pay him back the money she owed, right now, or his finance company would send in the bailiffs.

"What are bailiffs?" whispered Val. "What does that mean?"

"They come to your house," said Mum, in a dazed voice. "Bailiffs. They can take everything you've got, and sell it to get the money you owe. They'll take the cars, the furniture, the carpets, the kitchen fittings. Our clothes, our jewellery. None of it belongs to us now, love ... the bailiffs will have to take it. Oh, I'm so sorry."

"Can they take *Nippy*?" Val asked in a shaky voice. She felt like a little girl in a nightmare. She could see these horrible big men, grabbing her cat, and the kittens ...

"*No*, love," said Mum. "No, they won't take our Nippy."

Val started to cry. "Oh, Mum." Mum held out her arms. Val held on to her mum, as if she was a little toddler again. Mum rocked her, whispering, "My little girl, I'm so sorry, I'm so sorry—"

"I know what to do!" said Dad, suddenly. "You wait there, Jackie."

Dad went off to the kitchen. Val got up slowly. Did Dad really have the answer? She had a wild hope that he would come back with a huge stash of money, a suitcase full of five-pound notes that he'd been saving up.

Dad came back with a tray. On the tray, on one of the best plates, was a beautifully-made sandwich, with a tasty little salad on the side.

"There," he said. "I made you a nice tuna-mayo sandwich, Jackie. It's got chopped red pepper in it. That's Charlie's latest combo, and it's very tasty. There's a drizzle of walnut oil on the salad. I know you like that."

Mum stared helplessly at him. Dad took her hand, and kissed it.

"Listen, love. It's bad news, but it's only money. The house is still in my name. I'll apply for Income Support. We can get the mortgage paid that way, so we'll have a roof over our heads while we work out the rest. We should thank the Lord we like nice cars better than fancy houses, eh? We're lucky! We didn't move to a posh house and take out a fancy mortgage. We can sell the cars right away. Easy come, easy go, that's what I say.

Now, eat up. You haven't eaten all day.
I know what you're like when you get tense."

"You're so good to me, Tony," croaked
Mum. "I don't know what to say, the way
you've taken this. You're the best husband in
the world."

Like a hero, Mum ate the whole sandwich,
though Val knew it was choking her. She said
it was very tasty, and that she felt much
better.

"We've got each other," said Dad. "And
three kittens! Come on, Jackie, come on, Val,
let's have a break. We'll go and play with the
kittens and see what's on the telly."

But Mum gave Val a secret, scared look as
they left the dining room.

Oh boy, thought Val, *there's more!*

It was a strange evening. Val kept looking
at things, and touching things, thinking, *That
doesn't belong to us. The bailiffs can take it*

*away. The big flatscreen TV. The CD and DVD
player. The smart gold velvet curtains.*

My clothes don't belong to me!

She couldn't look at the statue. But she
could feel those red eyes staring at her.
Cassandra had won. Doom had been foretold,
and doom had fallen.

Doom and destruction.

At last Val went to her room. She got
ready for bed and lay there, too upset and
scared to think. She heard Mum and Dad
come upstairs. She heard them talking softly
as they went to and fro to the bathroom.
Then the door of their room closed.

About an hour later, Mum knocked on
Val's door and came in. She sat on the end of
Val's bed. She was wearing her white silk
kimono. Her dark curly hair was tied up and
her face was as pale as paper. She looked like

a Roman lady from Cassandra's time. She had a tragic, terrible story written in her eyes.

"Your dad's asleep," she said. "I can't tell him, Val. I can't tell him the worst, not yet. But I've got to talk to someone. You're too young. I shouldn't tell you, but I've no-one else."

"What is it?" whispered Val, her throat dry with fear.

"What I told you both, about Mr Marcos, that's only the beginning. When I had money, I used to like gambling."

"*Gambling*?" Val thought of Mrs Pritty. "Do you mean card games?"

"No, horse races, mostly," said Mum. "I never let you and Dad know, but I didn't see any harm. It was just fun. I had an arrangement with the man from the dodgy mobile phone shop. He put the money on the races for me. I paid him back and gave him a bit extra when I won anything. Only, when I ran out of money, somehow I stopped winning."

"But you didn't stop gambling?"

Mum hung her head. "That's right. I was trying to get back on top."

The "dodgy mobile phone shop" was a scruffy little shop near the old market in town. It wasn't really called the "dodgy mobile phone shop". It was called *Connex International*. There was a sign outside, offering cheap rates on calls to other countries. But the police knew all about *Connex*. Val had heard that what *really* went on there was stolen phones and illegal gambling.

"I owe a lot of money in gambling debts," Mum went on. "You just don't know, Val. I know I was in the wrong, but you don't know how debts can mount up and get out of control. I kept pretending everything would be OK."

"How much do you owe, Mum? Tell me."

"About a hundred thousand," said Mum, with a gulp.

"Oh my God."

"The man at *Connex* says I owe him a hundred thousand pounds," repeated Mum. "His name is Akili. I don't know his second name."

"But ... but can he prove it? Do you really owe him that much?"

"I don't think so, Val. But there's nothing I can prove. It was all cash, and word of mouth. And texts and e-mails. I've got no paperwork. It's like the money I owe to Mr Marcos and his finance company. When you owe money to people, they find things out. I think the man from *Connex* knows *Floral*

Magic's gone bust, and he wants to grab whatever I've got left.

"I've been getting phone calls. They scare me. They're really nasty, and … and I'm going to have to go to the police. I'll have to get a lawyer, but I think I'll end up in prison, no matter what."

"Oh, Mum!"

"You see, I've been gambling illegally, Val. There's fraud, too, things I didn't tell you but Dad knows. That I did to hide my debts." Mum looked at Val. "I know I deserve to go to prison, and I'll take what's coming to me. But I hate myself for doing this to you and Dad and our families. My poor dad, your grandad, it'll kill him."

My mum's not going to prison, thought Val. *I don't care. I won't let it happen*. Then something came into her mind. She drew a deep breath.

"Mum, I want to tell you something ... it's going to sound stupid and weird."

Mum wiped the tears from her face. "What?"

"You know the statue I found? The one we took to the museum? It's kind of magic. She's called Cassandra and she was a princess from Troy, I think that's somewhere near Greece. She could tell the future. Only no-one believed her, so it was a curse. Anyway, if you touch the statue, a voice speaks in your mind. It's happened to me twice. She foretold that the white kitten would die, and she foretold ... something that happened to Nessa. She speaks of hidden things, Mum. It says so, round the edge of the shield. *Rei Obscurii Dico.* The man in the museum told us."

"What are you talking about, Val?"

"You see, I was thinking about Nippy, and she told me about the kittens. If you touch

51

the shield, thinking about all that's happened, Cassandra might tell you something that will help us."

Mum stared at Val. In the end, she shook her head. "I don't understand a word you just said, sweetheart. But whatever it is, I'll try it."

They tiptoed downstairs, and switched on the living room light. Nippy sat up, and watched them from the kitten box. Mum opened the display case. Cassandra's eyes had a dull glow, like dark, shining blood. Her mouth with its bandage looked like a prison for horrible secrets.

"What do I do?" asked Mum, looking worried.

"Put your finger in the mouth-hole in the plate, that's her shield. And think about the debt and everything."

"I can't stop thinking about it," said Mum.

"Oh, and say we believe in her. That might help. The curse was that no-one would believe her. I think that's why her mouth is gagged – no-one would listen."

"I believe in you, Cassandra," said Mum.

She touched the hole in the stone shield, and a look of amazement came over her face. Her hand dropped down to her side. She stared at Val with her mouth open.

"What did she say?" asked Val. "What did you hear?"

Mum stared at Val and spoke in a voice that was not like her own.

The visitor with gold rings

Holds the fate of this house in his black box.

The enemy flees, the trap is set, the brave risk all to gain victory.

But fear comes.

Peril and fear.

Mum shook herself, and blinked.

"What did that mean? All those things I just said?"

"You heard the voice say all that?" asked Val.

"Yes," said Mum. "But what does it mean? It doesn't make any sense."

"Yes, it does," said Val, with a frown. "I think I get the idea."

Chapter 5
The Briefcase

Val thought about telling her dad. But she knew why her mum had chosen to talk to Val about the really bad part of her story. They both loved Dad very much, but they knew he was *useless*. If Dad knew a ruthless criminal was telling Mum that she owed one hundred thousand, he wouldn't have a clue what to do about it.

It was up to Val to find the answers.

She got Mum to write down what the statue had said, and thought it over carefully, until she was *sure* she understood. It was like a code. The visitor with gold rings was Mr Marcos. The black box had to be the briefcase he always carried with him. "The fate of this house" meant there was something in the briefcase that would save Mum. Maybe something that proved she didn't owe so much money. If Val got it back, the finance company wouldn't be able to send in the bailiffs.

They'd still have to deal with the man from *Connex* and Mum's gambling debts, but sorting out Mr Marcos would be a start.

They had to get hold of that briefcase.

Mum and Val got together in Val's room the next day, when Dad was out at his part-time job in the town hall. They made a plan.

Everything was still terrible, but it felt better when you were fighting back.

"Do you know *exactly* what Mr Marcos's briefcase looks like?" asked Val.

Mum closed her eyes, and thought hard. "Yes," she said firmly.

"Good. The first thing we have to do is get one just like it."

"We can do that. I know where to buy one. There are lots of briefcases like that in the shops."

"The next thing is, do you know when Mr Marcos's birthday is?"

"His *birthday*!" Mum's face went pink and her eyes flashed. "Why would I know that? He's not a friend of mine. Of course I don't!"

"All right, all right," said Val. "All I mean is that 90 per cent of people use their date of birth as the code on their locks. I read that."

Mum looked at Val in amazement. "I'm learning about you," she said. "You're quite a girl. I wish ..." She shook her head. "I've been somewhere else. I've been thinking of nothing but my debts ... I've missed my baby growing up, and I didn't even know it. That's a brilliant idea, Val. But what if his date of birth doesn't work?"

Val had thought it all out.

"The best plan is to switch briefcases. We'll take the letter or whatever papers we need, and then switch the cases back again. If I can't open the real case, then we'll keep that one and break it open to get the papers out. After that we'll get rid of it. If the finance company *is* cheating, Mr Marcos won't be able to complain even if he thinks we took the case."

"How will you know what to take, Val?"

"I'll look for your name. I'll take any papers with your name on."

Mum didn't look at all sure. "I don't know what else to do," she said at last. "And I heard that voice in my head. This is crazy, but let's do it."

Mum phoned Mr Marcos and asked him to come round again, right away. She made a bit of a mystery of it, and that hooked him. He said he would come round first thing in the morning. That was the only time he could make it. Then Val and Mum went out and bought an identical black briefcase.

The next day, Val watched from her bedroom window, and saw the big dark car arrive. She'd bunked off school, which wasn't like her at all, but this was an emergency. Dad was at the town hall, and wouldn't be home until lunchtime.

She saw Mr Marcos coming up the front path, gripping his briefcase under his arm, and clutching the handle as well. *I hope he puts it down indoors*, she thought. *The case looks as if it's glued to him.* She heard Mum saying hello. There was a long wait. Val moved to the top of the stairs, where she would be ready to move fast. The dining room door opened, and Val heard Mum's voice, loud and clear.

"Come into the kitchen, Costas, and we'll have coffee. May I call you Costas? I feel I'm losing a friend ... what a shame, when we're getting to know each other. You've been *so* good to me."

Huh? thought Val. *Losing a friend? What's that about?*

She dashed down the stairs as quietly as she could, holding the new briefcase. She'd put some newspapers into it, so the case wouldn't feel empty if Mr Marcos picked it up before she'd put the old one back. She picked up the old case and ducked into the living room. She hid behind the door. She heard her mum and Mr Marcos going back into the dining room with their coffee. Val could see part of the display case on the other side of the living room. Cassandra was looking the other way, so Val couldn't see the bandaged mouth or those grim red eyes.

The dining room door opened again.

"Just a minute, Costas. I'll fetch the cream, I left it in the kitchen."

Mum poked her head round the living room door.

A whisper came, "6-3-65." And Mum was gone, back to keeping the enemy busy.

You are a hero, Mum, thought Val. *You're a total hero.*

Val dashed up to her room, clutching Mr Marcos's briefcase. She shut the door behind her. Now, everything depended on Cassandra.

Cassandra said the answer was in here. In this case.

At least, that's what Val hoped the words had meant.

6-3-65. She twisted the numbers on the lock into place.

The case wouldn't open. Val began to sweat. Then she worked it out. If it was his date of birth, it could be 06-03-65. She tried again, with all six numbers lined up. The lock opened. Val pushed back the lid of the case, and her mouth dropped open.

The briefcase was *stuffed* with money.

Stuffed to the brim with pink fifty-pound notes!

She was meant to grab a vital document, and sneak downstairs again. Then she would hide in the living room until Mum came out with the empty coffee cups. Val would give her the thumbs-up. Then Mum would get Mr Marcos out of the dining room on some excuse, and Val would switch the briefcases back ... That was the plan. Now Val just stared at the money.

She slammed the case, spun the lock, and shoved it under her bed.

My God, she thought. *What am I going to tell Mum?*

Minutes passed that seemed like hours. At last Val saw Mr Marcos go. He had picked up the briefcase he thought was his own, and was holding it as if it was the most valuable thing on earth. Now Val knew why. She hurried downstairs, as soon as she'd seen the car drive off. Mum was looking very shaken. "Couldn't you get it open?" she said at once. She didn't wait for Val to answer. "That's bad. I tried to keep him talking, but it was no good. He had a plane to catch. Now he's going to open that fake case and ..."

"I couldn't help it, Mum."

They sat at the dining room table. Val put her head in her hands, thinking hard. She felt as if her head was going to explode. All that money! It was Mr Marcos's job to go round collecting cash, but it couldn't be normal for him to carry that much money.

"Mum, why did he want you to pay all of your debt all of a sudden?"

"It was in the letter. I don't really know ... it was such an awful shock. I'll have to look again. It takes time to understand a letter like that."

"But was it a proper letter from the company?"

"The letter had a company address at the top," said Mum. "But Mr Marcos gave it to me himself. He said I should give *him* all the cash I could pull together, and he'd try to hold the company off. But I think the statue might be right. There's something funny going on, Val. This morning Mr Marcos wasn't worried about getting the money. He just wanted to know what I'd meant when I said I had to see him at once. When I said I only wanted to talk to him, he seemed very glad."

"Oh boy," muttered Val. "Oh boy ... Mum, I've got to go out. I have to hide the briefcase somewhere safe until we have a chance to ... to break it open—"

"But Mr Marcos might find out he's got the wrong case and come back any minute! We should open it now!"

"It'll be OK. He's got a plane to catch. Got to go, Mum!"

Val took all of Dad's treasure-hunting gear out of his kitbag. The briefcase fitted into the bottom, out of sight. When Mum saw Val wasn't going to change her mind, she didn't try to stop her.

"You've got to trust me, Mum."

"I *do*, Val," said Mum, and gave her a hug.

Val got the bus to the golf course. There were people on the greens, busy playing golf on this sunny day. Val took the footpath round the side. She walked fast. Only the other night she'd found out that her family was broke, and nothing they owned was really theirs. Now she had more money than she'd ever seen in a bag on her back. She reached the treasure hunters' clubhouse, unlocked the padlock on the door with Dad's key, and slipped inside. The hut was dark. It smelled of the camper stove and damp. Without the treasure hunters there, it was almost spooky.

She set the case on top of an old box, and opened the lock again. No, she had not been dreaming. The money was still there.

She picked up one of the slim bundles and looked through all the notes. It was amazing. There could easily be a hundred thousand in here! *A hundred thousand pounds.* Her head was spinning, full of mad ideas.

The door creaked. Val jumped. She span round, and there was her father, staring at her. There was no time to shut the case.

Dad had seen what was inside.

Chapter 6
The Set-up

"I came up here to have a think," said Dad, handing Val a mug of strong, sweet tea, made with tinned milk.

He sat beside her, on a box that had held lawn feed, and grinned. "I've got something different to think about now."

The black briefcase lay on top of the old box. The lid was closed, but to Val it felt as if pink rays from those bundles of money were shining out of it.

She leaned back in the old deck chair she had found, and closed her eyes. So much had happened, she was trembling. But she felt calm inside, here with Dad.

It was like being in the still centre of a storm.

She had told Dad everything now. All about Mum and the gambling debts. How they had stolen Mr Marcos's briefcase, hoping to find something that would save Mum from going to prison.

The only thing she hadn't told him about was Cassandra. She couldn't talk about magic statues, not on top of everything else. It was too much.

She hoped Mum wouldn't be angry that she'd told Dad about "Akili" and the nasty phone calls from *Connex*. But she had a good feeling that it would be all right.

The family was in this together, and they'd support each other.

At least there was that.

"Mr Marcos is on the run," she said, and took another sip of sweet hot tea. "I think he's robbed the finance company, and they were going to find out. That's why he decided to grab as much cash as he could, and get away fast. That's why he told Mum last week that she had to give the money to *him*, personally.

"This morning, when she rang, he was scared she might have found out something. He had to come and see her, even though he was off to the airport with all his loot."

"I think you're right," said Dad, nodding. "It's something like that."

"We'll have to give the money back to the finance company, won't we?"

"I suppose so. I'll have to think about it. But for now, let's make sure it's safe." Dad looked thoughtful.

He moved the stacks of *Metal Detector* magazines from under where the map was pinned up. He rolled back a piece of old mat that covered the floor of the hut, and shifted two planks.

There was a dark space underneath. "This is the secrets hole," he said to Val. "We don't show it to outsiders, but I reckon even Scottish Dave would agree you're one of us. We've never had any secrets to keep in it, yet. But it shows how these things come in useful."

He put the briefcase in the hole, and put everything back the way it had been.

"We'd better get home, love. Your mum will be worried sick."

Val had come to the treasure hunters' hut to hide the money. Now that Dad had done exactly that for her, she was scared.

She wondered what his plans were.

Mr Marcos did not come back. Two days later, Mum got a letter from the finance company – in the post, this time. It said Mr Costas Marcos no longer worked for them, and any cash Mum had given him in the last week did not count as a payment to the company.

There was a statement of Mum's account, showing how much money she owed. It was awful. There was another warning, too, about the bailiffs.

Mum rang up the head office, and talked to someone who told her more of the story. Val had been right.

"Mr Marcos" (if that was his real name) had gone, and they'd found a lot of money was missing. The company thought that he had left the country.

Mum hadn't wanted to tell Dad the other half of her terrible story. But now that he knew everything, she was glad. She said she and Dad would take over, they would deal with things somehow, and Val should just try not to worry.

Val was scared Dad was planning something mad, and that her mum was so desperate she wasn't going to stop him.

But what could she do? All she could find out was that Dad had called in the treasure hunters to help. There was someone on watch, hiding in the bushes up on the golf course, night and day.

"Just in case," said Dad. "After all, a hundred thousand pounds is a lot of money."

Val didn't get much schoolwork done, and Nessa kept moaning that it was like being friends with a zombie. She didn't even want to play with the kittens.

One day, a week after Mum and Val had taken Mr Marcos's briefcase, Mrs Davis, the games teacher, even sent Val home early. She said Val looked as if she was coming down with 'flu. Val let herself in, and walked through the house. Dad was in the kitchen, chatting to someone on a mobile. She heard enough to make her creep up very softly.

"2 a.m. in the Blue Room," said Dad. "I want you all there. Got that?"

Then he grunted, as if someone on the line had asked a stupid question.

"Yeah, I'm talking about the Marcos money. What else? The hot stuff. We need to get it spread around, put in different places, before anyone knows we've got it."

Val backed away. She kept on walking softly backwards, right back to the front door.

She felt behind her and opened the door, then slammed it.

"Hi! Mum? Dad? I'm home! I got let out early."

Dad came to meet her with a big smile that gave nothing away, and hugged her. "Your mum's having a rest. The kittens are playing hell in the living room, and I bet you're hungry. How about a sandwich? I can do you a hard-boiled egg and sun-dried tomato?"

He still had the mobile in his hand. It was a smart little phone, except it was *pink*. Had Dad chosen a pink phone for himself?

"What's with the phone, Dad? I don't think I've seen that one before."

"It's nice, isn't it?" said Dad. He flipped the phone open and shut. "I picked it up at the old *Connex International*. You know, we have to watch our pennies now. In fact, my

74

mates all got phones, too. Dirt cheap phones they have down there."

"Dad, I know you're planning something. *Please*, tell me ..."

Dad shook his head. "I'll make you that sandwich."

Val went into the living room. Owl and Fawn were jumping along the top of the pale leather sofa, spitting at each other. Nippy sat on the flower-pattern Chinese silk rug. She was waving her tail, so Checkers, the black and white kitten, could play with it.

Val stared at the gleaming black statue in the display case. *The Marcos money ... 2 a.m. in the Blue Room ... We need to get it spread around ...*

"What on earth is going on?" she whispered.

No voice spoke in her mind. Cassandra stared, with her eyes looking like blood above

75

her bandaged mouth. Val didn't dare to open
the glass door, and touch the shield.

Chapter 7
The Sting

Val went to bed early that evening. She didn't feel ill. She just wanted to be alone so she could think. What could Dad be doing? She walked up and down her room, wishing she had asked Cassandra ... but she didn't want to know what new disasters were about to happen. She thought about what she'd overheard Dad say to his mates. It sounded as if Dad was planning to meet the treasure hunters, in the middle of the night, and share the money out between them. But why would he be doing that? It didn't make sense.

"They're just like kids," she muttered. "Just like crazy kids ..."

She lay down, and the stress of the last few days took over. She fell asleep at once, as if someone had hit her over the head.

A few hours later she woke up. She was lying, fully-dressed, on her bed. The clock on her bedside table said it was midnight, and, all at once, the thoughts that had been going round and round in her brain before she fell asleep made a clear pattern.

She sat up, gasping aloud, "The phones!"

Dad had said he'd bought his new phone from *Connex International*. And the treasure hunters had all done the same. But those phones were dodgy. They were stolen, they'd been fixed. Val was sure that when anybody used the phones, the bad guys could listen in! Val knew that these things could happen. Dad was such a dreamer, he hadn't thought of it. And he'd been *talking about the hot money*, talking about his daft plan to be out in a field with it in the middle of the night. He was too dozy to work out that the criminals, the people who Mum owed money to, could be listening.

Oh, Dad, you're a grown-up! How could you be so—?

And then her blood ran cold.

Her dad wasn't so dumb. It was worse than that. He had used the dodgy phones on purpose. He wanted the bad guys to know.

Suddenly, she noticed that the house felt very silent. She flung open her bedroom door and ran downstairs.

"Dad? ... Mum!"

She was alone in the dark house, except for Nippy and the kittens, and the statue of Cassandra. Her dad must already be on his way to the Blue Room.

But where was Mum?

Fear follows. Peril and fear.

Val would have called the police, she was so scared. But she didn't know how she would explain about the hundred thousand pounds of stolen money. Instead she rang for a taxi, and asked the driver to drop her off near the Blue Room. She had a torch with her, but she didn't need to use it. There was a bright moon. She went as fast as she could to the big field, the Blue Room. If Val was there, Dad wouldn't be able to do anything mad. He'd have to listen to her. He'd have to take her home.

When she got to the field there was nobody there. The bare earth was hidden now, under a thick carpet of young wheat. The branches of the trees above the hedge were covered in leaves. Everything looked cold and strange in the moonlight. Val didn't know what to do. It was quarter to two. Where were they all? Then she heard the noise of a powerful car, and a big jeep came up to the other end of the field. Val saw two figures jump out and open the gates. The jeep came through.

Val was sure that wasn't the treasure hunters. She didn't have much time to think. She scrambled onto the gate where she'd been sitting the day she'd found Cassandra, and jumped from there up into the branches of an oak tree. She felt safer when she was off the ground. But the jeep didn't come any closer. It stopped just inside the field, the Blue Room, with its lights turned off.

Charlie Woo was the first of the treasure hunters to arrive. Then came Kerry and Big Sal, and Mrs Pritty with Old Scottish Dave. Last came Val's dad, and her mum with Young Dave. Val could see them from her hiding place, but in the moonlight she couldn't make out everything. She couldn't see their faces. Mrs Pritty and Scottish Dave were carrying something big. She couldn't tell if Dad and his friends had noticed the jeep, which was hidden in the dark shade of the wood. She knew she should shout, she should warn them ... but somehow she couldn't.

She had to see what would happen.

They stopped at the gate, right under Val's oak tree.

"OK," said Dad quietly. "Everyone knows what to do."

"Righto," said Kerry. "Don't you worry, Tony. We're solid."

Val's dad had the briefcase. The big thing Scottish Dave and Mrs Pritty had been carrying was a folding table. They set it up. Mrs Pritty stood a bright camping lantern on the table. Dad put the briefcase down beside the light, and opened it. It looked as if they really were here to share out the money. Then the jeep started up. It crossed the field, and three men got out. To Val they looked larger than life, they looked like monsters. Two of them carried big flashlights.

Kerry, Sal, Charlie Woo, Val's mum and Young Dave melted away into the shadows of the hedge as the three men came up. Scottish Dave and Mrs Pritty stayed with Dad. The man who wasn't carrying a flashlight must be the "Akili" Val's mum had talked about. You could tell by the way he walked that he thought he was really important. He came right up to Val's dad.

Akili wasn't as tall as Dad, but to Val he looked very scary.

Dad shut the case, but not before Akili had had a good look.

"What are you doing here?" said Dad.

"So you're the guy," said the man who must be Akili. "I've been wanting to know more about you, Mr Hector. You and your fun and games. And your wife. I know Jackie well."

"Leave my wife out of it," said Val's dad, staring at a gleaming gun that had appeared in Akili's hand. "This is between you and me."

"Oh, but she's not out of it. Your wife owes me a lot of money."

"That doesn't matter," said Dad. "I'm not even going to argue. It doesn't matter because you're finished. I have the London mob ready to back me up. I knew you'd come here tonight. Think again, Akili, old son. I laid a trap, and you've walked right into it."

The word "trap" must have been the signal. Suddenly Val's mum, Young Dave, Sal and Kerry and Charlie all moved in together, and made a half-circle around Akili and his guards. Mrs Pritty and Scottish Dave stepped forward, so they were on either side of Dad. Val let out a whimper of horror. Dad's friends had guns! Young Dave had a shotgun set against his shoulder, Mrs Pritty was holding a pistol ... Kerry had her knife, and *Val's mum* was pointing a shotgun at Akili, a shotgun with a sawn-off barrel.

This can't be real, thought Val. *This can't be happening!*

Now there were eight people against three. Akili's guards reached inside their coats.

"Don't do that," said Dad calmly. "You might get unlucky."

But Akili's eyes glittered in the moonlight, and Val knew he wasn't going to back down. "Things go my way here," he said. "Your goons won't shoot, and we both know it. So hand over the Marcos money, and everything will be fine."

I've got to call the police, thought Val. *Call the police!* She scrabbled for her phone. Everything went upside down. Val fell, with a

wailing cry, through the branches. She
landed in a heap on top of the folding table,
which collapsed and threw her at Dad. Dad
went flying, knocking Mrs Pritty's pistol out
of her hand. Akili grabbed the black case, and
jumped back.

"All right, Mr Hector," he snarled. "We'll
call this quits. For now."

He and his guards ran back to the jeep,
got in and went roaring away across the field.
Val sat up, feeling dizzy and very confused.
Her mum helped her to her feet.

Kerry gave a whoop, and did a short
victory dance. Charlie Woo took off the
stocking-mask he'd been wearing and mopped
his face.

"Well, that was very exciting," said Dad.
"Shame about the money, but never mind,
can't have everything. Easy come, easy go.
C'mon, let's get out of here."

The treasure hunters' hut felt warm and safe. Mrs Pritty put the kettle on, Young Dave got out the mugs. Scottish Dave took out a bottle and had a small nip of whisky. Normally he kept off the drink when he was with his friends, but nobody said anything.

Val sat staring at them all. She couldn't believe what had just happened.

"Well," said Dad, "I'm sorry. I did think of just giving him the money."

"I thought of that," Val admitted. "I know it's not ours, but it seemed like that was what we were meant to do." She wasn't going to explain about Cassandra.

"But if we'd given in too easily, he might have just come back for more. It's greedy people who become criminals, isn't it? So I thought, better if *he takes* the money. And thinks he's taking it from another gang."

"People know about us, you know, Val," said Charlie Woo proudly. "They think we might be a gang. The police have had their eye on us before now."

"Because they don't understand what we're doing," explained Young Dave. "We're out and about at odd hours, we have secrets, and weird gadgets."

"And you talk in code," put in Val's mum. "You could well be crooks."

"So we bought the dodgy phones, and we set it up," finished Dad.

Big Sal nodded at the stack of weapons lying on the pile of *Metal Detector* magazines. "The guns are ours," she explained. "We *like* guns."

"Some are really old and some are models," said Kerry. "We collect 'em. They've got no firing pins, Val, they can't shoot. They're harmless. Not like my knife."

"But we *looked* dangerous, didn't we?" said Scottish Dave.

"You falling out of the tree wasn't part of the plan," said Young Dave. "That was a great touch, it made it easy for us to let him get away."

Val thought of the treasure that might still be buried where she had found Cassandra. Tonight, the site of the Roman ruins might have been covered with blood.

Doom and destruction.

She gave a shudder as she thought about what might have happened.

But the brave risk all for victory.

Dad put his arm around her shoulders.

"It's over, love. And no-one got hurt."

"You're all c-crazy," Val had been so scared her teeth were still chattering. "You could have got yourselves killed. *Their* guns weren't fakes!"

"No, they weren't," said Dad grimly. He looked at Val's mum. "It was a terrible risk, Val, and I'm not saying we did the right thing. But we were desperate."

Val's mum leaned over, and gripped Dad's hand. "It was all my fault, Tony. I know it was."

"I don't see that, Jackie. I got the flash car and the holidays, didn't I? And all the other stuff. I never said, 'Let's slow down.' I never said, 'Where's all this money coming from?' I liked the good life, same as you did. While it lasted."

Mrs Pritty poured the tea. "Well," she said, "as long as Jackie has learned her lesson, and turned her back on evil gambling, that's the important thing. Old Dave, where's that bottle of yours? I think we could all do with a drop of something in our tea."

Chapter 8
The End

The dodgy phone shop closed. Val went to have a look, and there was nothing left but an empty shop. Even the *Connex International* sign had gone. Someone at school said the *Connex* boss had been tipped off that he was going to get done by the tax office, and that's why he'd vanished. More likely, he was off somewhere spending the money he'd taken from the treasure hunters.

For Val and her mum and dad there were big changes. They kept the house, and Mum found work. But the two cars had to go, and all their smart things.

Val had to learn to live with the pity in people's eyes, and the way they talked about her family. She had to live with never having new clothes, or any money for treats.

But Nessa was still a true friend, and they still had Nippy, and young Fawn, and, of course, none of it made any difference to the treasure hunters. If ever Val felt hard done by, she just had to remember that night in the Blue Room, and how it could have ended. Then she knew she was very rich, and very, very lucky.

The Roman villa under the fields of Seven Hills Farm turned out to be real. But, apart from Cassandra, there was nothing valuable. There were no hoards of coins, no gold and jewels, only the bare, burned-out bones of a home that had been stripped of everything, in some long-ago disaster.

The treasure hunters moved on to other sites. Cassandra herself ended up in the town's museum, in a display case all of her own. Sometimes Val started thinking about everything that had happened, and she was afraid it couldn't be over. "Akili" would come back, demanding more money ...

Then she would go to the museum, and look at the Trojan princess.

But no voice spoke in her mind, ever again.

Barrington Stoke would like to thank all its readers for commenting on the manuscript before publication and in particular:

Claire Baines
Sarah Bevan
Sam Bridges
Susan Brougham
Kate Elliott
Adam Hayward
Tracy Hirst
Andrew Lindsay
Rob Lyons
Michael Marshall

Ben Morrissey
Thomas Nicholls
Joshua Nightingale
Emily Pidgeon
Shaun Rankin
Sam Robinson
Sue Robinson
Rebecca Shaw
Ruth Snipe
Edward Yerburgh

Become a Consultant!

Would you like to give us feedback on our titles before they are published? Contact us at the address below – we'd love to hear from you!

Barrington Stoke, Sandeman House, Trunk's Close,
55 High Street, Edinburgh EH1 1SR
Tel: 0131 557 2020 Fax: 0131 557 6060
E-mail: info@barringtonstoke.co.uk
Website: www.barringtonstoke.co.uk